CURSE OF THE HOLIDAYS

VOLUME 1

DEAD SNOW

JOSHUA C. FULLER

CURSE OF THE HOLIDAYS

VOLUME 1

DEAD SNOW

WRITTEN AND ILLUSTRATED BY

JOSHUA C. FULLER

CORRUPT HEART STUDIOS

iUNIVERSE, INC.
NEW YORK   BLOOMINGTON

Curse of the Holidays
Volume 1: Dead Snow

Copyright © 2009 by Joshua C. Fuller.

All rights reserved. *No part of this book may be used or reproduced by any means, graphic, electronic, or mechanical, including photocopying, recording, taping or by any information storage retrieval system without the written permission of the publisher except in the case of brief quotations embodied in critical articles and reviews.*

This is a work of fiction. All of the characters, names, incidents, organizations, and dialogue in this novel are either the products of the author's imagination or are used fictitiously.

Corrupt Heart Studios
Huntsville, Alabama, USA
www.CorruptHeartStudios.com

iUniverse books may be ordered through booksellers or by contacting:

iUniverse
1663 Liberty Drive
Bloomington, IN 47403
www.iuniverse.com
1-800-Authors (1-800-288-4677)

Because of the dynamic nature of the Internet, any Web addresses or links contained in this book may have changed since publication and may no longer be valid. The views expressed in this work are solely those of the author and do not necessarily reflect the views of the publisher, and the publisher hereby disclaims any responsibility for them.

ISBN: 978-1-4401-3768-6 (pbk)
ISBN: 978-1-4401-3770-9 (cloth)
ISBN: 978-1-4401-3769-3 (ebk)

Printed in the United States of America

iUniverse rev. date: 4/16/2009

CONTENTS

Ch. 1

In the Beginning

There is only Light and Dark. This story I'm about to tell you is not one of just Vampires, Demons, or Angels, but of all of them together. You see long, long ago, before life was the way it is now, before humans stood and walked the earth, the universe was very different. Billions of years ago, when life as you know it was still in the process of being created, there were three great gods.

The first was Sky Seraph, the Angel God, a being of pure and just intentions who wanted nothing more than to please the angels he ruled and ensure their lives were filled with happiness and peace. On his body where the marks of light, the sign that he truly was one with the light as it seeped from the marks. He was the wielder of the White Rose, the sword of light, a weapon of pure light that he used to give his world, his people, that peace.

The second was Vars Blood, the Vampire God, a lustful, yet elegant and peaceful being who took the lives of his vampire brethren seriously. Yes, he had a love for blood, but he made sure that his kind, though demonic in nature, were higher and stronger than even the most horrifying demons. Just like all Vampires, he covered his eyes, but since his stare was so much more horrifying than the rest of the vampires he ruled, sunglasses were not enough. His eyes were more terrifying than the worst of demons so Vars completely hid his eyes from the world with a blindfold. He wore a sword of beauty on his hip, the Red Rose, the sword of blood. This sword held in it both the pains and the strengths of all that he had loved and lost, making it also known as the sword of love.

The third god, Vars' brother, was Donovan VonBreak, the Demon God who cheated his way into power. He was a horrible being who tormented and destroyed an entire planet to push his brother off the throne. Donovan was a creator of pain and grief. He took all that he could get his hands on and turned it into nothing but a dark, corrupt form of living evil. He twisted the land he controlled to a wasteland of dust, fire, and metal. On his back, the Black Rose, the sword of darkness, a sword made of pure darkness in the form of black steel. It was his most cherished possession that never left his side. Not many know how he came to possess it; however I am certain we will know someday.

These gods were the rulers of two worlds, a world of light and a world of dark. The world of light was home to only angels, and peace was their treasure. It was a world of lands covered with beautiful forests, of lakes and mountains, and of crystal cities gleaming in the light. With the other world lingering in the darkness of space, the angels grew in peace and strength every day, all the while hoping that the other world would stay where it belonged.

The world of darkness was a treacherous and dangerous world filled with destruction and constant war. It was covered with rocks, black hills, and mountains as sharp as razors; the sky was always dark, and rarely was there a day it did not rain. In this world, life only existed if the gods were so lenient as to let it. This dark world, a battleground, was home to both the ever-elegant vampires and the horrifying, death-loving demons. This world was the essence of pain.

The beings of both worlds never really thought about each other. For decades it was this way, until one day, after vampires and demons had finally made peace with each other, the demon lord set his sights on some place new; a world that glowed and shined in space like a star that would not die. He hated the light and wanted it to end. With the help of the vampires, the demon god Donovan grew not only stronger but also smarter. Locked away for no eyes to see, in the forbidden archives, he found a spell. The spell was one of dark intentions and corruption... his favorite. The monster Donovan took forth the spell and plunged it into his soul, making it the key that forced worlds to become one, and kept them that way.

In the world of light, without warning, a black pearl-like planet plummeted at them from the sky and crashed into the world of light slowly twisting it and pulling it into itself. The angels quickly, and as planned, went forth and struck down all the demons and vampires they could. For several years, things began to seem like the light was winning, but the dark never let up.

Then something happened the demons did not expect. An angel and a vampire, as they crossed both gun and blade, found that they could not kill each other, but felt love towards one another. These two great beings were my parents. My mother, Lilly Seraph the granddaughter of the Angel god, and my father Larcuss Redfang, the grandson of the Vampire god.

They first met each other in battle. Lilly was conducting an assassination at the Black Tower research facility with twenty of her best swordsmen by her side. Larcuss had been assigned by the gods to protect the target with ten of the Elite Guards.

The angels snuck in swiftly and quick. They slipped through the rusted, blood-covered walls in dark halls and made their way toward the Black Tower to reach the target. They came across a laboratory, finding wings pinned up on hooks and bodies of dead angels piled in the corner of the room. Lilly had two of her men plant bombs around the building as she and the others moved forward.

The vampires stood lingering in the dark, waiting for the angels at the top floor. Slowly and quietly, the angels reached the top without being spotted by the scientists. As the angels opened the door, they discovered it was a trap. The vampires struck the door open with their weapons at the ready.

"Sorry to disappoint you, but you're not going any further," Larcuss spoke, reaching for his guns.

The angels, committed to their mission, moved forward to kill. Lilly pulled out her sword, a gift from her father, and Larcuss pulled out his guns, hand crafted by the vampire lord himself. They clashed hard, Lilly striking swiftly as Larcuss burst forth, shooting with precise aim. Lilly dodged, cut, and deflected every shot as Larcuss sidestepped, jumped, and dropped, dodging the razor sharp blade. As their allies died around them, they fought hard and long. After an hour of fierce fighting, they were all that was left of both sides, yet they could not find a weak point on each other.

They both were taught to perfection and they proved to each other that there was no way they would give up. Soon they started to talk. Asking each other why they were fighting, breathing hard from exhaustion. Nearly in unison, they both answered, "Because it's for what's right and just."

Perplexed, they both cautiously pulled back and put away their weapons. Surveying their dead comrades, they wondered if it was really worth it. Larcuss asked why she was after the target and what she knew about him. Lilly replied saying that the target was a grand demon, one of the spell keepers for what holds the worlds together. She had been told the target was one of the high demons who not only was one of Donovan's closest, but also had tortured and killed both angels and vampires to run his experiments.

When Larcuss heard this, his face twisted with anger and pure hatred. He bowed to her and took her hand in his. "My dear you may have given me the one piece of information that will change everything." He turned pulling out his guns. "Now how about we take out that evil wretch and stop this madness."

She smiled and moved up next to him, unsheathing her blade, "May we stand firm and strike hard."

They darted forth and burst through the door to find that the demon god had a different plan. The target stood before them, but not alone. The great demon god had twenty of his secret police protecting the target. They were horrifying putrid beasts, appearing small and weak as if they were diseased, with sickly pale skin, armor, and a mask that crushed the skull with in it. Their flesh was deformed and riddled with decay, like a dead body. They looked almost as if they could die at any moment. These ill looking creatures then morphed into the ultimate demon bodyguards. Their bodies transformed showing their true forms. Their masks split open revealing layers of fangs dripping with drool and stomach acid. Their arms throbbed as their muscles felt life in them again, thickening as they released blades from under their flesh. They looked as though they would become giants as they grew, straightening their backs and legs. Then they gave out a horrifying scream and lunged forth.

Lilly and Larcuss stood their ground. Larcuss shot rapidly into the bloodthirsty creatures. Lilly charged forth, cutting through and knocking away all in her path, Larcuss finished them off as he followed blasting open their skulls and chests. Suddenly, just as she thrust her blade with the intent of wiping that fat disgusting wretch out of existence, one last guard stood in her path striking away her blade. The creature then threw itself at her, its blades aimed right for her neck. With swift movements, Larcuss, in the blink of an eye, appeared above them shooting the creature's blades away as they shattered into shrapnel and turned the monster itself into a liquidized pulp with a barrage of bullets.

They regained their ground and glared at the demon that stood ready. It wore an unusual machine-like suit with two huge, long arms that had all manner of torture and surgical tools on the ends. He swung his arms at them like a crazed animal as they quickly dodged, jumping back. They glanced at each other and grinned, then charged at full speed. Larcuss ran ahead, shooting the pressure hoses for the limbs, stopping the demon's movement. Lilly slipped in from behind and sliced the limbs clean off. The demon fell back hard. He started to panic as he unhitched himself from the machine and tried to waddle away.

Lilly rushed forward as Larcuss jumped and flew over her. She struck the demon hard repeatedly as Larcuss shot him, filling him with lead. Larcuss landed on one side, Lilly on the other. Lilly's blade glowed blue with light; Larcuss' gun glowed red with darkness.

In perfection, they struck. Lilly thrust her blade in deep, twisting it upward in the demon's stomach, as Larcuss shot a curse shot down into his skull. As the opposites, light and dark, touched they forced the demon's body apart causing him to

8

explode; turning him into nothing but a giant bloodstain on the room.

"Finally...this disgusting wretch is finished...and I now have you to thank for it" said Lilly, relieved catching her breath.

"Oh no. It is you who must be thanked. If you had not come along, the treachery of the demons may never have come to me. This will change everything between our two races." They looked into each other's eyes. For the first time they were glad they didn't kill what got in the way of their goals. Slowly, they grew to love each other.

Soon after the Black Tower fell, the peace between the demons and vampires was broken and the peace between the angels and the vampires began. This threw the demon god into a hateful frenzy. He mobilized all manner of demons to him, demanding them to come forth and serve him or die. During this time, the vampires and angels grew together and found that they had a lot more in common than they realized. They vowed to wipe all demon life from the worlds. As a celebration, my mother and father, Lilly and Larcuss were wed in the name of the gods, in the name of peace, and in the name of their love.

For years, it seemed like the darkness wasn't even there. The peace between the angels and vampires grew stronger and unstoppable as the gods stood side-by-side watching over them. However, things were very different with the demons. For 50 years, the demon god gathered and strengthened every demon that came to fight. He studied the vampire and angel races, waiting and planning for just the right moment to strike, to cripple them into submission, and take control over both worlds.

At this time, Lilly Seraph and Larcuss Redfang had two children, Drake age forty, and me, Cloud, age thirty-nine. I had a family of my own, my wife Sonja, my oldest son Cross age twenty, my oldest daughter Rossa age nineteen, my youngest son Shade age fifteen, and my newborn baby girl Aria. We all lived in peace for 50 years.

But, among the Redfang family, there grew suspicion. After a while, it started to seem as if my brother Drake and my son Cross were disappearing more often each day. At first, we thought they just went hunting, or patrolled the border a little more than other guards. They would disappear for weeks, then suddenly be back without saying anything to anybody about where they went or even acknowledge that they were ever gone to begin with.

I went to my father to ask for his advice in hopes that he would have an idea or opinion to this strange behavior. I went before him and bowed showing my respect, "Father... I come to you because I expect you have the same suspicions as me... I know it's been decades since you and mother killed the disgusting meat bag and brought peace between the races, but it seems that not only my brother but sadly also my own son may have betrayed us and may be working for the enemy."

My father looked at me, my mother at his side. My mother responded, "Son we know exactly what you mean, your father and I, as well as the gods, have been suspicious."

I looked at her surprised, "The gods?! I didn't realize the situation was that bad."

My father replied, "Yes son, there have actually been several missions to find out what they have been up to, but every time we send someone out they don't come back. It seems that whatever Drake and Cross are up to, they have gained enough power to both keep our people off of them and not leave any evidence behind."

I sat there thinking and surprised, "We must apprehend them at once and question them of their motives, why they have betrayed us."

My father objected and stopped me "No son! I am sorry to say this, and I really mean that, but they have gone too far. It seems that there's a possibility that we may be too late."

My mother stood and went to the steel, sacred cabinet, "My son, under these circumstances we must insist to the gods that we attack first. Your father and I will go and speak to them. But before we go, we have gifts for you," She pulled her sacred blade from the cabinet and offered it to me, as my father offered me his guns.

"Free Light and the Hell Raisers? Mother... Father... I can't accept these."

She replied, "Son of course you can, these are yours now. You use these with honor and make us proud. Take these weapons and use them to defend our people just as your father and I did."

I took them, rising to my feet, "Yes... I won't let you down."

My father smiled, "Now go. Apprehend Drake and Cross as soon as possible and if there's no other way... you must kill them."

"Yes sir!" I said with hesitation. I turned and in the blink of an eye, I was gone, moving as fast as I could, strapping the sword to my back and the guns to my sides. At the same time, Lilly and Larcuss went to the Temple of the Gods to tell them the time has finally come to take out the demons before they take us out.

Ch. 2
Sibling Rivalry

I rushed down the alleyways of the twisted streets, heading straight for the Black Bridge to head off Drake and Cross before they got the chance to leave and tell the demon lord the last piece of intelligence about our defenses. I rushed as fast as I could between buildings, jumping rubble and walls. As I ran, I came across some of our scouts and asked, "What's the status?"

The head scout replied "We have managed to spot a demon frontal scout assault team marching for the Black Bridge, about 10 miles out.. From what we were able to see, behind them was what looked like the whole demon army. Their scout team spotted my men and I. They attacked and only three of us got away. I'm afraid the others were slaughtered."

I looked at him surprised and at the same time infuriated.

I gave him some adrenalin pills, "Go as fast as you can and inform the gods of what you know." They saluted and darted away as fast as they could for the Temple of the Gods. I worked my way to the bridge. I finally got there and stood in the center as Drake and Cross arrived.

"What do you think you're doing…?" I asked as I glared at them.

Drake replied with a deep evil laugh, "We were offered true power and a place as ruler over two of the new worlds."

"New worlds? There are no other worlds but this one," I said.

He laughed again, "Oh little brother... And to think, you became a Captain of the Shining Blood Army...a master of both gun and sword..." He sighed staring at me. "Now is the time for you to leave my sights for good," He glared at me as a black flame grew in his palm.

I looked, watching the flame grow. "That's not angelic or vamperic power...how?" I said as I reached for my sword.

"This is just a sample of the power that the demon god as gifted to us...now, my brother, you shall die. Cross," he spoke and drew his black blade, "continue on ahead and join up with our lord, tell him of the plans."

I yelled, "Drake don't do this! You're betraying every one that has ever cared about you, everyone who ever trusted you."

He laughed once more, "Trusted me?! No one ever trusted me! No one ever cared! Now, everyone will DIE and this world will be under the rule of the real king and ruler, Lord Donovan! Cross, get a move on!"

Cross replied with a "Yes!" as they lunged forth at the same time.

I pulled my gun and blade. I aimed for my son Cross, hesitating at first, but then right as I pulled the trigger, Drake blasted the gun from my hand with a ball of black fire. I turned and clashed Drake's blade with mine. A black light glowed in his fist; a burst of black fire erupted from his hand as his fist made contact with my stomach. I could feel the burn dig deep into my flesh, and my skin scar with pain like nothing I've ever felt before.

I quickly pushed Drake back, gasping for air. "What the hell was that?!" I held my gut as the burns tingled and surged with pain.

Drake laughed. "That's the power of the black flame brother and believe me those scars will never go away."

I glared at Drake as I stumbled to my feet. "You think that power is the better? Well how about I give you something you won't ever forget!" I held my pose, my blade Free Light glowing with a bright shining light.

The look on his face proved that he knew what he was up against. "Mother's sword I see . . . and I assume you also have Father's guns as well. I guess this will prove more challenging than I thought." He then forced the black flame power into his blade, mutating it into a great steaming black steel blade.

I charged at him, and he at me; we clashed blades hard. Sparks of light and darkness dripping off the blades like acid, burned our flesh and the ground around us. At the same time, without realizing it, we each saw an opening on the other and struck, slashing at each other's chests. The force of the contact caused us to fly apart from each other.

As I struck the ground, I blacked out, darkness filling my sight... I heard a rough voice "Don't give up, keep moving, don't stop." When I came to, I saw that my brother was down and still out. I stood to my feet, still feeling the burning pain in my gut. I walked over to take his sword, when a dark cloud turned the sky pitch black. I looked up to see that it was moving.

"Damn!" I said as I turned to see hordes of demons swarming behind me, just rolling over the hills, and pushing through each other to get to the bridge first. I rushed over with both guns in hand, shooting down every demon I could and holding them back. One after another, they rushed me trying to get across. I stood my ground shooting brains out left and right, stopping each one from crossing the bridge.

Soon, I was covered with the putrid, disgusting black blood of the demons I slue. Larger ones charged me with blades in hand. I dodged hard, their blades just missing me, but I was slowly opening the wounds Drake had inflicted. I put one of my guns away, grabbed my sword from the ground, and shredded through them, my blade sending them back to the darkness from which they came. For every one I cut or shot down, ten more rushed to cross the Black Bridge. The ground started to shake as the greater demons ran on to the bridge. In one slash, I cut them down, but no matter how many I removed from existence, they kept on coming.

I took a breath and rushed through them, amputating and dismembering all in my path. When I reached the end of the bridge, the demons backed down ever so slightly. My body was covered and soaked in their putrid juices… my burns felt like they were going deeper and deeper. I glared them down, them screaming at me, getting ready to charge me again.

Then, without warning, a demon of great stature jumped through the darkness behind them and struck at me repeatedly. I dodged as many blows as I could and tried to shoot, but in one thrust, he knocked me back, slamming me to the ground.

I slowly began to lose my strength, my muscles ached and my wounds bled and burned. I pointed my blade up, the monster of a demon knocked the blade from my hand and laughed horrifically as it raised its blood stained club. I raised my gun with my last shred of strength, aimed and shot him right between the eyes.

The hordes charged again, screaming. As they came closer, a black figure appeared in front of me, as if he was there this whole time. He spoke two words, "Blood Grim-row" and in one sweep shredded the demons crossing the bridge. The demons still on the bank looked at him in astonishment, as did I. He turned toward me, "My name is Victor VonBreak and from this day forth, I am your ally."

The demons hissed and growled at him, "You traitor! You will pay for betraying us!" They screamed and charged us. He turned slashing them back, then picked me up and rushed us away.

"What the hell do you think you're doing? Without me guarding that bridge, the demons will get across and will swarm the land!" I yelled, not knowing his intentions.

Victor snapped back, "Do you have any clue to the kind of injuries you have? With those burns, you're lucky you've lasted as long as you did. If I hadn't shown up when I did you would have been dead and I'd be going this fight alone, so shut up and be thankful."

I looked at him, "Whatever you say man…" I reached into my pocket, pulled out an adrenalin pill and ate it.

He looked at me, "You better make the best of those things. With those injuries, you would be out for days without those pills."

I glared at him, "Who the hell are you anyway?" I pulled my gun pressing the barrel against his head.

He looked at me replying "For now that doesn't matter, all that matters is that I am a friend and I don't care if you like it or not. I'm going to help you. Now get your gun out of my face…"

I stared at him unsure as I put it away, "I still don't trust you but I guess I have no choice but to accept your help… we need to go to the Temple of the Gods!"

He quickly replied "It's too late, by now the demons are swarming that area and the gods are fighting as we speak…" I looked at him surprised and shot off as fast as I could for the temple. He watched in amazement "Damn, I need to get me some of those pills."

CH. 3
THE END

War broke out around the temple as demon, angel, and vampire clashed and ripped at each other with tooth, fang, blade, and gun. As we raced to them, a dark figure suddenly flew overhead. A monstrously large shadow, covered with a black shade of clouds and smoke wrapping it, flew over us. As it flew, I could see the temple fall. The angel and vampire gods rising from the smoke, drew their swords and destroyed all demons who tried them. The angel god Sky and Vars, god of the vampires, then turned their attention to the darkness flying towards them and raised their blades.

"Shine and cast down evil!" yelled Sky.

"Taste blood and love!" roared Vars. Their swords transformed as they slashed through the smoke to see Donovan emerge, his sword shining with a dark flame as it mutated into a huge black blade.

"Long time no see Vars. And the ever so grand angelic god Sky Seraph. I never expected your people to have such strength! But today, there will be only one god and that will be me." Donovan laughed as the black flame flowed out his hand.

"Donovan..." Vars glared "How dare you use my people's magic for you own gain and then torture and experiment on them like they were nothing but swamp rats with no meaning! You will die for what you've done... I swear it..."

They raised their blades and rushed Donovan. Sky taking to the air, raised his sword and dove at Donovan, striking with amazing speed. Vars cast a gleaming red gun from his blade and shot furiously into every opening he could get. With amazing strength, Donovan pushed, clashed, and deflected every hit and bullet thrown his direction.

"How is he so damn strong!?" Vars exclaimed.

"Forget about strong, he's just as fast as me!" Sky yelled, striking as fast as he could. Suddenly, Donovan struck Sky hard with the face of his blade, hurdling him through the air. Donovan turned to Vars, his hand blazing with the black flame and cast at him one blast of fire after another. Dodging franticly, Vars jumped the blasts moving closer in.

"Hold the hell still!" Donovan yelled. Vars quickly shot at Donovan managing to get an opening, putting a bullet in his arm "Ah!".

As fast as he could, Sky sped at Donovan, slashing and cutting furiously. Sky thrust his blade forth. Donovan yelled, "Back off!" as he punched Sky's blade away followed by a kick to Sky's face. Vars dropped as Donovan spun suddenly, swinging his black blade and just missing the top of Vars' head.

Vars laughed lightly, "Missed brother." Vars raised his gun as the blade passed overhead, aimed right at Donovan's neck, and pulled the trigger.

Donovan quickly flipped back as the bullet skinned the top of his chin and kicked Vars away. Glaring as blood ran off his face, he replied, "Seems you missed, too." Donovan charged raising his blade.

Vars quickly rolled as the blade slammed down next to him "Too close!" He aimed the gun and shot franticly at Donovan. Jumping back, Donovan turned the face of his blade towards Vars. His bullets hit the blade and the fragmented pieces exploded as they fell to the ground, knocking Vars backward into the remains of the crystal building.

Sky flew in, as fast as a star, blasting Donovan through the building and pinning him to the ground. Sky held him down, his blade to Donovan's throat, "You're nothing but a filthy demon bottom-feeder that only managed to gain power by stealing the magic of the Vampires. I assure you that even if it's not by my hand or his, you will be cast back into the darkness where you were born. You will spend eternity as nothing but a body, hanging by your neck for what you have done to our people!"

23

Donovan glared, pushing him back slowly, "Bottom-feeder you say? You don't even know of the power I possess just by holding this sword!" He thrashed Sky back and slashed hard and fast.

Sky blocked and held the strikes as best he could, "The sword you say? I always wondered why there were two gods of the Dark world." Sky pressed him back, his blade gleaming with a blue shine, "I bet you stole it."

Donovan laughed, "No, but I sure as hell killed a lot to get it! It's not stealing if you take it off the dead!"

Donovan kicked the shining blade away then slammed the black sword down on it. Sky blocked, sliding the black blade off, and quickly slashed and gouged Donovan's stomach. "AHH!" he bled badly. "Ahh!… you mudak…you'll pay for that!" Donovan raged and knocked the blade from Sky's hands. He grabbed Sky by the throat, lifted him up choking him, "Say hello to your tribe for me."

As Donovan choked Sky, he charged a bolt of black lightning in his fist. "I hope this burns you more than it kills you!" Donovan laughed raising his arm. Then with perfect aim, Vars shot two piercing bullets through Donovan's arms.

"AH! Damn! Come on!" He dropped Sky, clenching his arms. Sky grabbed his blade, kicked Donovan to the ground, summoning his strength, he stabbed his blade through Donovan pinning him to the ground. "AH!" Donovan began coughing up blood.

Sky raised his hand to the clouds, "Light blister and pierce! End this madness!" Blue light electrified in the clouds and burst from them. Shooting down into Sky's hand, the lightning charged getting hotter, turning from blue to white hot, shining in his hand. He then clenched it, forcing it through his body and sword, into Donovan's body.

Donovan screamed as it flowed through him, "AHH!"

Sky then flung Donovan into the air, "Vars now!" Vars charged his gun as he raised it and blasted a blood red ball of fire at Donovan. Donovan fell to the ground, causing it to sink and crush him into a smoldering crater. Sky and Vars moved closer to the crater, "He better be dead now…"

Then before they could raise their blades, black fire shot from the crater, blasting them back. As they flew backward, Donovan appeared and caught them by their legs.

"How dare you! I'll make sure you both are nothing but rotting corpses when this is over! Now die!" Donovan yelled as he threw them into the ground creating more craters. He slammed his hands together. Sparks of black electricity flowed through and around his hands, "You call that pain, I'll show you pain. DIE!" Donovan faced his hands toward them, a slight pause filled the air followed by the black lightning erupting from his palms, sending death from above down on Sky and Vars.

Smoke filled the area, all manner of angel, demon, and vampire stood in wait. Silence… Donovan descended into the fading smoke. He listened for the slightest sound and laughed.

"This is too good; to think I not only killed my brother the blood sucker… but the angelic god of light, Sky as well. This is just too good!" Donovan laughed as he retrieved his sword. When he pulled his blade from a rock, the ground shook.

He heard a voice, "Killed?… You did nothing… You think you bested us? Well hear this, it's not over yet."

Suddenly, the smoke billowed from the craters as Vars and Sky rose from them, their forms not what they once were. Sky turned as his blade twisted with light, swirling the blade into a razor sharp point, it's edge gleaming with white feathers. It's blue ribbon wrapped itself around his arm, claiming him as its master, the light wrapping him as if he was the embodiment of light itself.

Vars turned, his blade twisting with the gun creating a blood red trigger with saw tooth blade and bleeding handle. The blood raced up his arm, casting him in the form of a crimson demon, his eyes glowed a deep, blood red, as a rose vine wrapped around his arm.

Donovan laughed, "Why won't you die!" he growled "Do you think you're the only ones?!" He laughed as he raised his blade. Donovan slammed the tip of his blade to the ground and a burst of darkness engulfed him, mutating him into a grotesque being of true darkness. Spikes and thorns grew from the blade as its size grew and a strand of darkness attached itself to him like a lifeline. Horns burst from his back releasing poisonous fumes from the seams of his flesh. His body grew and scaled. Donovan laughed as he opened his glowing yellow eyes and looked to Sky and Vars. Time stood still as demon, vampire, and angel alike, took shelter and watched the great fight.

Donovan grinned as an armor like shell covered his mouth, "Ready or not… here I come."

All three clashed blades, slashing furiously at each other. Sky cast white fire as Vars cast red on Donovan, who just grinned. As the smoke faded, you could hear Donovan laughing. He shot from the smoke, tackling Vars to the ground, "Remember this brother?"

He smiled and stabbed his giant blade into Vars' gut, who screamed with an agonizing cry, "Ahh!… Yeah, but I remember it differently."

Sky darted over at high speed. Donovan kicked him away hard, "HA! I bet you never saw that coming."

Vars glared, coughing, "How did you survive that blast, it should have turned you into nothing but ash…"

Donovan laughed again, "It is amazing what you can learn from a book, especially when you've been studying for the past five decades! That's right, I'm practically immune in this form, and now it's time for you to die." Donovan plunged his sword once more to finish Vars.

Sky picked himself up and looked over to see Donovan standing over Vars' body, blood rolling off his blade. "Vars? Why you…Die!" Sky was enraged; the light shown off him with a bright fury as he attacked at amazing speed, sparks blistering off the blades. Sky lunged his blade forward and Donovan stabbed his blade into the ground deflecting Sky's lunge to the side. Quickly Donovan grabbed and lifted him by his throat once more, kicking the blade from his hand.

"This time no one will interrupt me" his eyes glowing a deep yellow as he tightened his grip and slowly dug his claws into Sky's throat.

Sky whispered through his grasp "Even though I may die, my tribe will have their revenge and you will pay for what you have done. I just hope they are merciful and don't stray from the light. Now get it over with!"

Donovan laughed, "As you wish." He stabbed his blade into the ground. As he raised his hand, a spark flashed, then a horrifying flow of black fire burst from his hand flowing up his arm as it grew. "Here you go, now die!" With a single stroke of his wrist, he raised his hand and the flow of fire engulfed Sky's body. In mere seconds, Sky was no more...

CH. 4

UNKNOWN POWER

"NOO!" Feeling a surge of rage course through my veins, I charged at Donovan with full force. I slashed furiously as that burning hatred and rage grew. In the blink of an eye, my blade was 10 feet away from me and my throat was in the hand of that mudak.

"Why are you trying to throw your life away so quickly?" Donovan looked over my shoulder to see Victor walking over, "Son...what are you doing here?" He held me tightly in his grip as my eyes glowed a bleeding red.

"Oh you know, joining my dad in world domination," Victor replied.

"Really? Well then, do me a favor and shred this whelp's throat. I need a break." Victor walked in closer reaching for his blade. Donovan looked at me and smirked "Just wait, soon enough you will be dead along with every little angel and vampire that rejects my rule. That includes your mother, your father, your wife, your kids, and every other being you have ever cared for."

At that moment, I don't know what happened. Next thing I knew I was seeing red all over, my muscles throbbed and ached with a massive surge of adrenalin. I looked at my hands and looked forward to see Donovan with his arm cut off and Victor looking at me. His eyes widened as he stepped back from the look of me.

I looked and saw my reflection in the remains of crystal on the ground. My eyes glowed and my body was changed. My hair turned a blood red as it thickened and flowed behind me. My skin was grey with a black mark growing down my face. My feet were cracking and arching up like Donovan's.

Victor looked at me, his eyes wide open as I looked to Donovan. Suddenly, time seemed to stand still as I rushed at him. I felt my nails thicken and stretch out like claws as I shredded Donovan's chest open. I could feel darkness flowing through my body and my hate grew as I slashed at him again.

Donovan cast his loathing eyes down at me, "You will not kill me, you worthless whelp!"

Donovan attacked, but Victor dashed over, stabbing his blade into Donovan's leg. "Gah!" he starred at his son… glared and knocked him away. "Not only has my own flesh and blood betrayed me but now this angel holds the power of both darkness and light! What the hell is going on here!?"

I spoke, unaware of how I sounded, "I am not just an angel but am both an angel and a vampire as one."

Donovan laughed at me, "This may be, but none the less, you two are out of here!"

"Why so?" Victor replied, wiping the blood off his blade.

"Because of this!" Donovan snapped his fingers as he mumbled something.

"No!" I yelled as I dashed and thrust my fist at his skull.

A barrier of some sorts stopped my fist and shot me back. He laughed and charged, in his hand a black pearl like a black hole. I ripped at the barrier as fast and as hard as I could but nothing worked. I picked up my sword Free Light, crafted by Sky himself, the essence of free, pure light. When I grasped it in my hands, it grew ugly and huge, spikes grew from it and as it turned into a grotesque dark blade, I felt a burst of hatred as darkness just flowed around me.

Donovan looked at me and laughed "It doesn't matter how strong you are you'll never be able to break through my barrier!"

In the blink of an eye, before he could finish talking, I charged striking my hardest slash against the barrier, knocking him back. Rocks piled up behind him as his body went limp, grinding across the ground. The only thing that ran through my mind was "Did I kill him?" The smoke faded as he climbed from the rubble, a twisting blackened yellow light wrapped up his arm and shine from his hand.

"I don't know how you got so much power so suddenly, but I'll make sure to get rid of you for good before you make the next hit. Now, let's see what this power is capable of, complements of the vamperic books of power." Donovan raised his hand over his head as the light shot from his hand forming a giant destructive orb.

I was horrified as I saw everything it touched vanish as it grew. I suddenly heard my name, "Cloud…" I look to see my family hiding behind some rubble and my dear wife Sonja crying, watching, scared, not of the orb but of what I was… I looked at Donovan as he laughed. I raised my blade and charged as fast as I could. As my blade made contact with his chest, I was sucked into the orb, blacking out as I went in… The last thing I could hear was Sonja calling out to me…"Cloud!" I fell into darkness and before I knew it I was in a completely different world…I felt so… cold.

CH. 5
A NEW WORLD

I laid there for what felt like hours… I felt so cold, so tired…
I felt like I was being carried away…many more hours passed.
I then suddenly felt life in me again, as if the light was flowing
through me again. I slowly opened my eyes and raised my head,
I could see someone through the haze "who's there?"

A tall figure stood and laughed lightly "Oh boy you sure are
a lucky one, if I hadn't come along you would have been a dead
man."

The voice sounded elderly and wise like my father but much
older. "Who are you and why did you save me?" I tried to sit up
but I didn't have enough strength.

"I'm sorry, my name is Samuel Wilson, but you can just call
me Sam. And you are?"

I managed to sit up. "I'm Cloud Redfang and why did you
save me?"

He laughed again, "So quick to the answer. Why wouldn't I? It's good nature to help someone and do what is right for justice. You know that."

The haze faded slightly as I could see a black coat and grey hair. Definitely an old man, had to be in his 50's or 60's. "Yeah…I guess you're right, now that one question is answered, where am I?"

He quickly replied, standing to go pour some drinks, "You and your friend are in my humble abode son."

I looked at him "Friend? What friend?"

He chuckled and pointed to a bed next to mine, "Your friend over there, he had some bad wounds as well but wasn't near as hurt as you. Yeah, he was out cold from being shook up, but you were strange. It was as if your life was barely hanging on."

I looked at him as my eyes finally fully recovered. He was a tall, lanky man with a small beard, long grey hair, and he wore a grey suit. "Well it seems I am in good hands then,"

I looked over to see Victor out cold on the other bed. As I took a breath, I suddenly felt a surge of pain hit me. "AH! What the…" I looked at my hands and then my body to see I was completely bandaged up as if I was burned and scarred all over. I wondered, was this from that darkness? Or from that yellow power?

Sam handed me something that looked like tea, "I'm going to go see if there is anyone else out there. Drink that. Should help."

He then grabbed his top hat that had a particularly strange skull on it and left. I looked around seeing that the place I was in was some sort of cave like cavern with a brick wall and door covering the exit. I tried to stand up from the bed but my legs were so limp I couldn't move them.

I looked at Victor, wondering to myself how he ended up coming with me. Did he try to save me and got pulled in too? Did he charge in after me just to follow? Or did Donovan throw that horrifyingly large orb of destruction and instead of killing us, teleported us? These things ran through my mind over and over as I tried to figure it all out.

Before I knew it, thirty minutes had past and Victor woke up moaning. "You're finally awake are you?"

He sat up glaring at me, "What?" He looked around, "Where the hell are we?"

I lay back down and sighed, "I'm not sure. All I know is that this is apparently a home or hideout of some old guy named Sam."

He looked at me, seeing me all wrapped up, "What the hell happened to you?"

"I'm not sure of that either. I woke up to find myself like this. I think it may have been from being pulled through that orb like thing."

He looked at me like I was an idiot, "I say it was from you losing it and turning into that ugly monster. Do you have any idea what you looked like turning into that beast?"

I looked at him, a little worried about what I had become. He continued, "You looked like you didn't care anymore, about life, about family, about anything. Your eyes had the biggest sign of blood lust I've ever seen. No demon has ever had that look in their eyes before. Not even Donovan."

I glared at him, forcing myself to sit up and reach for my sword propped against the wall, "That's right you're a demon… don't think I didn't hear you and Donovan talking. You're his damn son! What the hell are you doing this for? Why did you follow me through the portal? Why did you save me on the bridge? And why did you save me and betray your own father?!"

Victor snapped at me, "Shut up! I have my reasons, and as of right now I don't think it's something you need to know just yet."

I stumbled to the door and looked out a hole in the door to see a blizzard raging outside. "Well it seems we have plenty of time right now so spill it." He glared at me more. Before he said a word, the door burst open pushing me back as a dark figure walked in, pushing the door closed behind him.

"Oh, good gracious! Any colder and I would have been a frozen Sam."

Victor fell out of the bed trying to grab his guns. He quickly aimed the guns as Sam pulled the cloth off of his head, "Oh hold on now boy, I am no enemy, Sam is the name."

I sat up holding my back "oh hell that hurt! Yeah, he's the guy I told you about." Sam quickly helped me up.

I looked up to see that the cloth he had looked familiar, it was a black coat. "Sam? Where did you get this?"

He smiled, "Oh I found it out near where I found you two. I thought I might have left some other things of yours so I double-checked. Is it yours?"

"No… it was my father's. What else did you find?" He pulled from his pocket some sunglasses. I sighed lightly to myself, "Thanks Sam… I just hope everyone survived. I need to be alone." I put the jacket on and glasses in my pocket, as I walked out the door.

"No, stop boy! You can't go out there!" He chased after me, followed up by Victor, into the blizzard.

"Stop I said!" Sam grabbed my shoulder to stop me right as the snow stopped and the sound of a whip cracked overhead. We all looked to the sky to see a blood red sleigh fly overhead with a huge bag in the back.

"Ho Ho Ho! You actually think you could hide from me? I guess I'll have to give you a little extra treat for trying." The sleigh swooped back around, dropping sharp pendulums, cutting through the ice and snow. We all managed to dodge them. I pulled my blade but I couldn't hold it up. The more I tried, the more my wounds hurt.

Before I knew it, Sam pushed me, knocking me out of the way of one of the pendulum blades as it came back around. Victor shot at it furiously as I used my blade to force myself up. As it came at me, I used what strength I had to cut the cord holding one of the pendulums as Victor shot another. I collapsed to my knees as the blade shot off over my head and into the ice behind me, shattering it like flimsy glass.

A voice from the sleigh boomed, "Oh, you think you can stop the inevitable that easily? Well now you'll have to try on my claws!"

I looked at Sam as the man in the sleigh swooped down with giant hook like blades on the sides. I flung myself back and barely slipped between the blades as he shot past. I landed hard on my back, "Ag…Sam! Who the hell is that?"

As we ducked and dodged, Sam caught his breath and responded, "About two years ago a large group of creatures came to this world killing and enslaving everyone and everything they came across. I was here visiting the master of this land named Nicoli when the monsters attacked, and after a while they broke through our defenses and captured us. The last thing I remember is that a man bearing a black blade touched my head and then I blacked out. When I woke up I was shackled up against the walls of some kind of holding cell. I managed to slipped out of my chains and sneak out, and have been hiding out here ever since."

As I listened to Sam, he jumped at me, "Look out!" He pushed me down and dropped as the blades nearly scalped us. "Pay attention! The man in that sleigh is the King, you must not kill him!"

I pushed myself back to my feet. "Then what the hell do we do?"

Victor yelled running over to us. "Damage the sleigh,"

Sam said. "It's like a pet to him. But you have to do something really powerful son, bullets don't work."

I thought about it and then I had it. "I need my guns, where are they?"

Sam, irritated, repeated himself, "Son I told you bullets don't work!"

I yelled, "Where are they?"

He sighed, "Back inside on the table."

I hopped to my feet, "Thanks. Give me cover. I'll be right back." I rushed for the door as Sam pulled a large gun from his jacket and shot at the sleigh with Victors help.

"Alright old fart, I'm coming for you!" Victor yelled, running straight at the sleigh as it flew down at him. Victor held his ground with blade at the ready, and in one swift spin sliced off one of the blades and kicked the king right in the face.

"AHH! Damn!" the king swerved and flew up high to get away. They continued to shoot as he ascended.

As I ran inside, Nicoli evaded the shots, pulled a large pod from the back of the sleigh, and launched a missile into the wall of the cave. "Cloud!" Sam and Victor yelled as the ruins collapsed. Sam and Victor glared and shot like mad men, skinning Nicoli's face and arms with bullets.

He laughed "Is that all you got?!"

I pushed my way through the rubble, putting my father's glasses on. I pulled one of the guns, smacked the gun against my leg charging it, and aimed for the rear of the sleigh. Sparks shot and spat as the power of the shot grew. I watched as he spotted me and flew off trying to make a run for it.

"Come on damn it! I won't let you get me!" he yelled. When the sparks went red, I fired a crimson beam into the sleigh blasting the back out, knocking it out of the sky in one blow.

Sam and Victor looked at me, "Cloud!" Sam ran over and hugged me tight. "Sam! Sam! I can't breathe man."

He laughed "I'm sorry son, thought you were a goner there!"

Victor walked over and punched me in the arm, "Oww! What was that for?"

He glared "For nearly giving me a heart attack."

I rubbed my arm and put my gun away, "You sure are bent on me being alive."

He laughed a little under his breath, "Let's just say things would be much harder without you around."

An explosion went off behind him from the sleigh. We looked at each other and laughed as the sleigh popped and cracked. Sam on the other hand, raced over to the crash.

"Sam? What are you doing?!" We chased after him calling his name, "Sam stop you fool, if he's not dead, you will be! Now get back here!" He didn't listen, he just kept running till he got to the sleigh.

Ch. 6

The Traitor

Sam slid into the small crater to the huge burning sleigh. Showing amazing and unexpected strength, lifted and pushed away the sleigh, to see if the king was okay. Checking the blood red king's pulse, "Oh thank goodness. As satisfying as that was, it was to close. He seems to be alive but unconscious." He glared at me slightly, "You kind of over did it son!"

I slid into the crater with Victor behind me, "Well sorry, I can't help it. Usually when guys are trying to kill me I take them down."

He got up in my face, "You still could have killed him! Even though his mind is corrupt, that doesn't mean that is who he truly is. He is still the King of this land, and in the end, is the only hope for every being in this land. You kill him and the entire land will go into chaos."

Victor interrupted "Would it really be any worse than it is now, with how he is?"

Sam said scowling, "Yes, of course you damn moron. Without him, this land will rip itself apart until there is nothing but darkness where this bright and proud land used to be."

I sighed under my breath, "There is no way we are going to win this argument, right?"

He nodded as he knelt back down to the king, "Damn straight son. Now shut up and help me carry him."

We grumbled as we helped pull the king from the wreck. Suddenly I felt something familiar. I stood to my feet and took a look around... "AH!" Suddenly my burns surged with pain. I quickly knocked every one away as that black fire once again clashed with my flesh burning me deep, "AAAHaaa!... .

"Cloud!" Sam yelled, staring as a shadow like body emerged from the mist in the distance, it's face covered with a black glass mask of some sort, and a large blade on his back. I looked hard, trying to recognize him as I fought not to pass out from the pain... "Who are you?!" I yelled holding my side.

The man laughed through his mask, "What's wrong? Can't recognize your own... brother?"

He lunged at us, pulling a black blade from his back and slashing furiously as he laughed. I quickly dodged every slash, the blade just missing. I jumped it as it swung under me and then kicked him hard in the face. "What the? You're supposed to be dead! I killed you on the bridge!" We swung back around as I pulled my blade and blocked, falling back from my injuries.

"Oh well, sorry to disappoint." Drake pushed hard as I slid along the ice, "Yeah you got me, you got me good, but just like you, I still survived." He laughed as he kicked me down. Victor shot as Drake vanished from sight, then appeared just a few feet away. I could hear the anger in Drake's voice as he spoke.

"I guarantee you won't have the opportunity again! By the next time you raise that gun, before you can shoot it, it will be pointed at your throat," he laughed once more.

Sam picked up the king to make a run for it. "Oh no you don't!" As he turned, Drake appeared in front of him, "Sorry gramps, you're not going anywhere!"

I quickly jumped between them stopping Drake's blade. I knocked him back as he swung his blade again, "Back off! Your fight's with me!"

He chuckled a little, "Oh, sorry brother. As much as I would love to kick your ass, there will be no fight here. You three are coming with me, and bring that fat blood bag." I stood my ground and held my blade firm, "There's no way we're going with you."

He laughed again, "Too bad, because you don't have a choice." He suddenly vanished. The next thing I knew, I woke up chained in a pitch-black room.

Ch. 7
Survive

While I was in the snowy desert, back home, things were getting worse... Sonja crouched down holding her baby close with her son and daughter in the darkness of the rubble and ruins. The demons were patrolling the area, looking everywhere for survivors. They could hear screams and shrieks of terror as more and more angels and vampires were found and killed.

Sonja couldn't stand it anymore, "Rose, you're the only one of us who's been trained in the vampire magic. You take your little sister and head north through the mountains. Shade and I will stay back and help as many as we can. No matter what happens, you keep moving. You understand me?"

She quickly spoke, "But mom, I can't just leave you two to fight by yourselves."

Sonja gently stroked her daughter's cheek, "We'll be fine. You just keep moving, and we'll be right behind you before you know it. I know you can do it. Stay strong and no matter what, don't look back." Rossa stared into her mother's eyes and hugged her.

Shade hugged Rossa, "Don't worry sis we'll be fine, just go."

She slowly stood up and pulled a charm from her bag. "Okay… you two make sure to be right behind me!" she smiled as she spoke. "Vislass…" using the charm to make her and the baby invisible, she snuck away.

Sonja looked at her son and kept her blade close, "Ready?"

Shade nodded and they jumped from the shadows onto two demons patrolling. Shade stabbed his blade into the demon's face as Sonja ripped through the other before they could say a word. Pulling the bodies into the dark, they slipped through the shadows, sometimes even hiding in plain sight.

They came upon a building where they could hear crying and slipped through a window. They snuck down the hall to see a large demon beating an angel to death as a young angel cried, chained to the corner, "No! Daddy! No! Get off of him or I swear!"

The demon laughed walking over to her. Grabbing her by her chin, "Or what? What could you possibly do to stop me? I mean look at you! You couldn't even lift a sword! What could you do? There is absolutely nothing I need to worry about that you could do." He grinned and licked his lips getting closer to her.

"Your right… you shouldn't worry about what she can do to you." The demon's eyes widened as he swung around. "And worry about what I will do to you!" Shade glared with glowing red eyes though his glasses and grabbed the behemoth by his throat.

The demon grabbed Shade's arm, gagging as he tightened his grip. "You know, there are not many demons I will actually choose to use this on, just because I find it a waste of time… but.." Shade said as he opened the wooden case on his back. "You have just earned it." Shade reached in and pulled out a claw gauntlet pulsing with darkness so strong it was leaking off the claws like blood "congratulations… now die…" Shade then plunged the claws into his gut and twisted them in his stomach, tearing him open.

The demon's eyes went white as they rolled back in his head, the pure darkness forcing itself through his blood like a poisonous acid. He gagged, slowly coughing as the darkness seeped up his throat and out his eyes, nose, ears, and mouth. Shade glared at him, gritting his teeth. Then Shade saw the child watching him. The demon started to get thicker as the darkness began to split his flesh open.

"Shade!" Sonja yelled as the body pulsed with the darkness. Shade looked back at the behemoth swelling and coughing. Shade quickly pulled the claws from his stomach, then kicked him into the darkness of the hallway just before he exploded, covering the walls in blood, guts, and putrid flesh.

The girl looked up at him, tears running down her face, amazed as Shade walked over to her and Sonja tended to her father. "Are you ok?" Shade asked slashing the chains, then putting the dark claws away.

"I'm fine, all thanks to you," she grinned, standing up into the light. "Thank the gods!" she wrapped her arms around him, hugging him tight. Embarrassed, Shade blushed slightly and held her trying to comfort her. Sonja said, "Shade this man is still alive, but not for long. His ribs are broken and have pierced his lungs."

The girl ran over to her bloody father and held him close to her, "Is there any way to save him?"

Sonja shook her head, "He has internal bleeding. He'll only be alive for a few minutes... I'm sorry dear." Tears pushed their way out of her eyes as she held her father in her arms.

The angel mumbled and held his hand out to Shade, "Young man..."

Shade got down on his knee beside him and took his hand "Yes sir?"

The man pulled him close, whispering into his ear "It's thanks to you that my little girl is unharmed. Please take good care of my daughter."

Shade looked down on the man, as he coughed up blood. "I won't let her out of my sight," Shade said proudly.

The man looked at his girl, took her hand, put her hand in Shade's, and smiled as he slowly faded away. The girl cried and held him tight. Shade held her as he looked at his mother.

The girl turned and clung to Shade, crying into his shoulder, "This just isn't fair…why did this all have to happen… first the Gods… then my father and friends…"

"Girl, we need to go now. There may be more survivors." Shade said as he held her head up.

She looked up at him wiping her eyes. "What will I do?"

He smiled and helped her to her feet, "You're coming with me. Your father asked me to take care of you and that's what I'm going to do." He turned and picked her up on his back. Sonja picked up her blade and followed Shade as he jumped out the window and snuck through the dark. The girl looked back as she clung to Shade, trying to hold back her tears.

Meanwhile, Rossa quietly ran through the rubble, sneaking by amazingly large hordes of demons, tossing sleeping bombs when the time called for it. Baby Aria slept soundly as her sister maneuvered them through Hell in the making and its demonic people.

She came to a bridge and shivered as an eerie feeling crept over her. She looked around to see a great fortress of a ship appearing overhead through the smoke and clouds. Her eyes widened as she quickly ran across the bridge into the darkness of the mountain.

She ran through cave after cave trying to escape the sight of the ship, knowing something bad was about to happen. As she ran through one of the caves, small demons seemed to emerge from them following her after each cave she passed through, "Oh great…"

She kept running as she reached into her bag and sleeves, tossing chemical bombs and potions behind her, blowing up and mutating the monsters into sand or freezing them alive. Every time she killed one, they grew in number, from three to twenty in under a minute. The more she killed the more they kept coming, getting closer, slashing at her with claws and small blades.

She wondered "how is it these things can see me, could they have some sort of heat vision?" Right then one jumped on her back, "Get off!" She swung her arm up, knocking the claws away and grabbed the little monster by its head, smashing it on the ground as she ran. Suddenly, after she was about five feet away, the demon blew up, the blast causing her to fly forward ever so slightly.

"No way! They're nitroglycerin based, too?!" She ran as fast as she could, throwing explosives behind her more and struggling to stay away.

Shade and Sonja saw the ship appearing overhead, "We need to go… now!" Sonja yelled.

"What about the others?" Shade quickly asked.

"Run now damn it!" she said, "If there was any one left, they got out on their own!" Sonja darted with Shade right behind her, the girl on his back, running as fast as they could to the mountains. They soon came upon the bridge and ran across as fast as they could. As they ran through the caves, Sonja got a bad feeling as they exited the first cave. They ran past a frozen demon and knew Rossa was in trouble. They ran as fast as they could while up ahead, the demons cornered Rossa in a canyon.

Rossa laid Aria on the ground behind her and put a barrier around her. She turned to the demons, pulling a short thin blade from her robe. "There is no way you're getting past me!"

She held her ground, waiting for them to make a move. Just as they lunged to attack, Sonja appeared in front of them. In one swift move she cut their heads off and kicked them away just as they blew up.

"Mom!" Rossa hugged her mother tight and gave her the baby. "Were you and Shade able to save anyone?" Sonja pointed behind her at Shade walking over with the girl on his back.

She looked at Rossa and smiled, "Yes. Sadly though, we only had enough time for one."

As Rossa went to greet them, a sudden bright green light glowed overhead as everything was slowly being pulled toward it. They looked around to see rocks flying into the sky towards the ship. Rossa asked, "What do you think it is?"

Sonja looked hard, her eyes suddenly widened as she grabbed Rossa. "We need to go, now! Shade get in that cave now!"

They ran for the cave. There was a sudden pull toward the light followed by a hard blast of wind as the ship obliterated the remains of the city, reducing it into nothing but a black crater. The shockwave hit and its wind blew them into the deep cave as the opening shook and rocks fell down closing them off from the outside.

Ch. 8
Must Escape

I felt a strong urge to kill, to maim, to destroy. I lunged back and forth in the chains as they tightened on my wrists and neck. I felt so angry, as if hatred was fueling my feelings and making me want so badly to kill. I yelled as I felt my blood surge through my veins, my eyes glowed illuminating the room with a blood red glow. I looked around to see nothing but blood and limbs piled in the corners of the room. I then saw Victor and Sam chained up next to me, "Victor! Sam! Wake up!" Then a massive surge of pain hit me all at once, forcing my body to change.

Victor raised his head and looked around "Oh great don't tell me… I'm home…" He looked over at me "Holy shit! What the hell are you!" he pulled back in his chains.

"Oh shut up! It's me, Cloud." He stared at me a little confused, "Cloud? What the hell happened to you? You look like a demon."

I glared at him, "There's no way. I'm an angel."

Victor smirked, "Oh yeah, an angel has glowing red eyes, black wings, is 8 feet tall and with arched feet like a gargoyle, and to top it off your scars are glowing blood red." I hadn't noticed my jacket and bandages were gone and I didn't know that not only my eyes where glowing red, but my deep scars were as well. I thought to myself… what is wrong with me…

I shook my head and got serious, "Forget about what I look like, we need to get out of here."

Victor rolled his eyes, "Why don't you go crazy like you did before and just rip the chains out? You already look the same as our captors, just a little bigger."

I answered, a little irritated, "Because I have no idea how I did this, or if I'll even be able to keep control of myself like this. I could end up killing you both…"

He rolled his eyes, "Just do it before we are all turned into something that resembles behemoth shit."

I snapped at him, "What makes you so sure I won't kill you right when I get free?"

Victor countered, "Because you managed to control yourself while we were fighting Donovan. And believe me, trying to cut off that arm should have been like cutting through cryonic steel with a butter knife, and you managed to not only knock him back, but left his arm in a pool of blood on the ground. Now he's going to have to get a bionic arm, and if rumors are true, that's going to hurt like razors digging into bone!"

I sighed to myself, "That sounds really great and all but like I said, I need to know how to do it."

Victor ran thoughts through his mind, "Well you have to be already half way there. You look like a terrifying demon with glowing red eyes and big sharp teeth, what were you thinking about?"

I thought heavily to myself, "I'm not sure."

He then reached out and punched me hard in the face. "AH! What the hell!" and I remembered fighting my brother. All the evil that he has done, my rage grew slowly. Wanting him dead so badly, wanting revenge for all the lives that had been lost in vain, all because of him. Suddenly my body hurt all over, my scars stretched, and my hair turned black as I grew. My feet arched ever more and claws reached out from them digging into the floor. My veins burned and pulsed vigorously as my muscles tore ever slightly as they grew.

Before I knew it I was nine feet tall and in one flex, I ripped the chains out of the wall, taking the wall down with it. Shocked, Victor said, "Holy shit man! Tell the whole place that you're breaking out while you're at it!"

I broke their chains and tossed Sam on my back. I spoke with a deep voice, "Shut up! Let's just get out of here!" I turned, broke the door down, and ran down the hall with Victor following closely behind me. We came upon a four-way hallway and slid to a stop.

"Which way? Victor yelled looking around.

I suddenly heard footsteps from two of the hallways. "That way!" I said, charging down it as Victor followed.

"Why this way?" Victor asked, keeping up.

"We're being followed; I heard footsteps charging down the other two hall ways. Somehow I was able to hear their footsteps."

Victor looked at me like I was insane, "You could hear them? I didn't hear a thing! Seems that form suits you."

I glared at him "Shut the hell up and just follow me." Victor punched me in the arm. "You know I couldn't feel that right?" I said.

He laughed, "Yeah, yeah, I suspected as much. None the less I still wanted to hit you…"

We charged down the hall. As we came upon a corner, we slid and turned to see a few very large, white creatures roaming across from us on the other end of the hall.

Victor's eyes widened, "They are huge…" The creatures turned and spotted us, their eyes glowing a bright blue. As they turned they roared, shattering various crystal mirrors and windows, and charged down the hall at us.

"Victor, take Sam and stay right behind me," I tossed Sam into his arms and charged down the hall. I grabbed a statue as I ran and threw it hard, knocking out the first creature. I took a deep breath as I clothes-lined the following two, slamming their skulls into the ice flooring. We shot down the hall and slammed into the corner as we turned seeing a big door.

Ch. 9

Still Alive

Sonja awoke in the darkness of the cave. She tried to stand, looking hard, stumbling as she tried to see. She felt around, trying to find her kids "Rossa? Shade? Talk to me please." Soon, she came to a drop off of a cliff, nearly falling off it, "AH!" She breathed hard stumbling away from the edge. Her breath heavy, "Shade! Rose! Where are you?" she concentrated as she tried to adjust her eyes to the abnormal darkness. She felt around more, hoping to feel her baby Aria, then suddenly saw red.

A glowing red from out of the corner of her eye... She found her sword and pulled it from its sheath as the light got brighter and turned to her, coming closer. She raised her blade and listened for the slightest noise.

"Mom?" Her eyes widened as they finally adjusted and saw it was Shade, "Mom? Oh good, it's you. Finally found you, are you ok?"

She smiled and hugged him tight, "Oh thank goodness you're ok and yes I'm just fine. Where are your sisters and that girl?"

Shade took her hand, "They are all fine, a little bruised up but fine. I have been looking and finding all of you one by one. I brought everyone to this one room in the corner of the cave. Over here." He gently pulled her through the dark to a large cavern filled with gold and platinum plated walls that reflected the light from his eyes illuminating the room. Shade pulled his mother's hand gently and revealed the girls huddled by a wall.

Sonja grinned running to her girls, holding them tight as the other girl ran to Shade holding him tight, burying her face in his neck. Shade smiled lightly holding her and patted her back, "I'm sorry but in all of the commotion, I still haven't gotten your name."

The girl looked up at him, slightly embarrassed, "Its Ellen... Ellen Bright." She smiled, blushing a little, and buried her face in his neck once more.

"Ellen, that's a beautiful name," Shade said as he walked with her to the others.

Sonja held her baby close as the child played with her mother's hair. "Oh Aria. I'm so glad you're safe," she rocked her baby in her arms as she grinned and stroked the girl's hair. Rossa snuggled with her mother and sister as Shade sat and held Ellen close.

Rossa laughed looking at her brother with the girl, "Its amazing. From what I've heard, only two minutes of knowing her and you become her boyfriend."

Shade blushed as Ellen snuggled into him and laughed lightly with Rossa. He smiled and held her tight, "Well I must say, I'm grateful. When I went in that building, I didn't expect to have found her, but I'm glad I did." Ellen smiled big and held him tight as he laughed.

Suddenly a bright light shined overhead, "AH! Oww! Why so bright..." Shade quickly put his sunglasses on as everyone jumped to their feet, pulled out knives and swords alike, and stood their ground as the light came closer.

Ellen stood behind Shade, "What is it?"

It came closer and closer, then let out a sudden noise, "Meow." Their eyes widened with a very "what the heck?" look on their faces.

The light got even closer and went to the baby. Sonja jumped back and swung her blade. The sword passed right through the light as it floated to Aria. She smiled and held her arms out to the light as if she saw something that everyone else didn't. Aria giggled as the light enveloped her body and disappeared. Aria held it like she was giving a hug. "Meow." Aria laughed letting everyone relax, exhaling a very long held breath.

"Was that a demon spirit?" Shade asked as he put his blade away.

"If it was, then I doubt it was a bad one, or it would've attacked us, right?" Rossa asked.

Sonja looked at her baby and smiled seeing a shine in Aria's eyes, "Yes, it was a spirit… but it wasn't a demon spirit."

Rossa asked "Then what was it?"

Sonja grinned stroking her girl's hair "It was a guardian spirit. A protector, and it chose Aria."

Shade raised his glasses "It had to have dwelled here in these ruins for generations, the power it possesses is exponential. I'm really going to have to look into this more."

Rossa laughed lightly "That really would have came in handy outside when I was fighting off those little monsters. But oh well, at least she will always be safe, right?"

Sonja nodded. "Yes, she will never even get a scratch," she said stroking her baby's hair as Aria smiled up at her.

Ch. 10
Crimson Blood and Black Flames

Victor and I darted through the halls and finally, after working our way through the giant maze of a castle, came upon a big door. We knocked the doors down and ran into the huge crystallized room filled with art, weapons, and statues that looked strangely like bodies frozen in fear.

Victor said bluntly, "I guess we found our artillery." As we looked around, at the far end of the room we saw a large man in red, frozen solid, encased in a block of ice.

Right then, Sam woke up lifting himself from my shoulders. "What the hell happened?... Where am I?" He looked at me and fell back hard on his back, "Oh my sweet glory! Get back! Get back!" Fumbling, he reached for his gun to find it wasn't there, "Back you beast! Back!"

I rolled my eyes, "Relax Sam it's just me... Cloud. Am I really that scary?" I asked Victor.

"Yup, you remind me of my dad... Cloud why don't you change back already before you give the old man a heart attack," Victor said looking around.

"Yeah I guess. Okay concentrate... if rage made me this way..." I relaxed and breathed, thinking calm thoughts, about my family... Sonja...Rossa...Shade and Aria...even Cross, before all of this, when we were all happy. Soon, with a sigh of relief, my body regained its normal shape and I finally looked like me again.

Sam walked over to me and patted my back, "I'm glad to have you back son...sorry I freaked out there."

I felt so much better, "No problem Sam," I slapped his back in exchange and looked around.

"Now was that so hard? You seem to be getting the hang of that," Victor said as he looked through the various swords and guns on the wall.

He then spotted our weapons up on the wall like trophies "Hey Cloud, think fast!"

I turned to look at him as he threw me my guns and sword. "Whoa!" I caught them as they nearly made contact with my skull, "A little close?!" I exclaimed.

"Oh shut up and grab some ammo you big wussy," Victor snapped as he yanked guns off the wall. I glared at him trying to stay calm. I looked around but my father's jacket and sunglasses were nowhere in sight.

As Victor and I looked around, Sam walked over to the coffin of ice to get a closer look at this frozen man in red, to see it was the King. "Nick?" He asked with a hard sigh. "What has happened to you, my old friend?"

Victor and I looked through the collection of weapons and guns, grabbing anything that would help; shotguns, carbines and explosives. Victor dug around and came across something beautiful, "Oh yeah, a damn mini-gun!" He laughed, pulling it out of the cabinet and loaded it, grinning ear to ear.

I walked to over to Sam as I loaded the shotgun and placed it on my belt, "Don't worry Sam, we'll get him out of there. We just need to take care of someone first, to insure his safety."

Sam smiled as I handed him his very large gun, "I know son, let's go kick his ass. That brother of yours needs a well earned ass wuppin." He checked the gun for bullets and pointed it at the base of the great ice coffin as Victor joined us.

"Hold it right there gramps! Once again, he isn't going anywhere." We turned to see Drake and a man in a blood red robe.

"Drake…" I said, glaring at him as I cocked the shotgun.

Sam placed his hand on my shoulder, "Hold your ground son, no need for you to end up getting pulled into a trap."

Drake sneered as he pulled his blade from his back, "Cloud, you know it will take more than a few guns to beat me."

I laughed lightly, "Oh I know, but they at least make things easier!" I then aimed the shotgun at the man next to him and fired. They both jumped, vanishing and reappearing at the sides of the rooms. I looked close to see if I hit them. No marks on Drake but… the mystery man's robe was shredded, our eyes widened in surprise to see that the man was the King, the one from the sleigh.

Sam looked back at the king in the ice, then back at Drake, "What the hell did you do to him!" Sam yelled.

Drake laughed through his black mask, "To who? The fat man in the red is right there," he said as he pointed to the king in the ice.

"Just answer the damn question!" I yelled.

Drake then explained, "Well, you're all going to die anyway so… When I came here before, long ago, my associates and I, along with hundreds of thousands of demons, took over this land and infected its inhabitants. By forcing darkness into the King's soul, we intended to make him one of us…but… the light in his body rejected the darkness so much, it caused his body to force the darkness out, splitting his personality and body into two." Sam's jaw dropped.

Drake continued, "With this slight set back, we took what we got. I encased the king of this land in ice, while I made his dark side do my 'dirty work,' you could say, while I was gone. After the freezing of the king, I just left everything to the bad king. He killed, maimed, and slaughtered so many! He did quite a good job!" he laughed, looking at the Dark King as he grinned.

"Now it's time to take care of you once and for all, brother." He turned to the Dark King, "Kill the old man and black haired one, the other is mine."

The Dark King smiled devilishly and charged. "Ho! Ho! Ho! Here I come!"

I shot at him once more, knocking Sam away as the Dark King lunged at us and crashed into the crystal wall like a huge rock. I threw the shotgun at him as I jumped back; he turned and thrust his gut at the gun bouncing it off at me as if it was nothing. I flipped back as the gun flew past my head and I pulled the carbine from my back. I regained my ground, aimed and fired once more, just as Drake knocked the gun from my hands, slashing at me, missing as I leaned back, barely dodging the blade.

I quickly grabbed my blade and slashed up at his face with a hard swing. Luckily, my blade made contact with his mask cracking it slightly. I then spun hard in a buzz saw like form, smashing open the mask to reveal his ugly, scarred face. He stumbled back, holding his face. His eyes gleamed as he pulled the remains of the mask off, and threw it behind him as he raised his blade.

He glared at me as I stared at his scars, "It seems when I made contact with you on the bridge, I did more damage than I thought."

He ran his fingers along his face, "Oh yes, it seems you did, but I got you too," he said as he looked at all the scars on my body.

"I don't know how you survived, but I'll make sure you're dead this time," he ran at me, grinding his sword to the ground as sparks shot off with black fire. "I liked your form, now look at mine!" He slashed the blade up in front of him, spinning like a black fiery buzz saw, clashing hard with my sword as the black fire raged off the blade.

Victor kicked the Dark King hard in the side sending him flying into the crystal wall, then opened fire on him with Sam pinning him to the wall with a feast of bullets from the mini-gun till it was out. When the smoke faded, he was gone...

"HO! HO! Close, but not close enough!" He appeared right behind Victor, a very large gun to Victor's head. "You just got a chunk of coal up your stocking," he laughed horrifically and pulled the trigger.

"Not yet!" Sam kicked the gun away as it shot, obliterating one of the many frozen bodies. Victor pulled his blade and slashed repeatedly as Sam punched and kicked. The Dark King dodged and blocked really well for a big guy.

"Come on boy, your gunna have to be a little better than this to beat old Nicoli!" the Dark King said as he chuckled and kicked Victor away.

Sam glared and nailed him hard in the gut.

"AH!" he coughed and gagged as Sam twisted his fist in the evil fake's stomach.

"You are not the king... you're nothing like him! You can't even take a punch!" Sam yelled. With a burst of speed, Sam started beating away at him with a swift but strong series of kicks followed by a hard jab to his nose, breaking it.

"AH!" Sam then kicked hard nailing him in his stomach once again. Taking his boot to the fake's face, then using that force to crush his skull into the crystal ice floor.

"Almost there!" Sam took a deep breath for the finisher, he jumped hard to the ceiling sitting against it like a bat hanging from the top of a cave, then shot off like a bullet back down, slamming both heels deep into the Dark King's stomach.

The floor cracked and split. Sam stared at him, breathed deeply, stepped off, and walked back over to Victor. Victor, completely surprised, stood there with his jaw hanging, then shook his hand, "That was amazing Sam."

He chuckled. "Why thank you," Sam smiled shaking his hand in return, "No problem son, I did what I needed to do." Victor then squeezed his hand.

"Ah! Oww!" Sam yelled.

"Then why the hell didn't you do it sooner? Like when we were still out by the ruins?!" Victor asked.

Sam breathed a little heavy as Victor ground his knuckles a little, "I was tired and didn't want to strain myself, now let go!" Victor let go and Sam quickly slapped him upside the head "Respect your elders, damn it!"

Victor glared as they suddenly heard a grumble and a light laugh. Their eyes widened as they looked over to see the blood covered Dark King slowly standing back up.

"I'm still here boys…" he spoke as he coughed up blood, "… and I am going to kick your jolly asses." He laughed wiping away the blood and in the blink of an eye, dropkicked them both into the wall by the frozen coffin.

I clashed with my brother at screaming speeds. Drake swung his blade at me vigorously as I dodged every slash.

"Hold still damn it!" he yelled, once again jumping at me spinning like a black saw. I quickly stepped to the side and knocked him away as he shot towards me.

He slammed into the wall, breaking a hole in it. "How is it you're so fast?" he yelled glaring at me. His eyes glowed as his pupils turned from black to white, filling with pulsing darkness. "You are really starting to irritate me!" he slammed into me in the blink of an eye, knocking me into the wall with his blade against mine.

He laughed pushing harder and harder, "You know what? I bet your wife is in slavery right now cleaning and scrubbing the floors, bathing Lord Donovan with blood, being forced into bed!" I glared gritting my teeth.

He kept on, "And your kids made into nasty little meat pies for the demon lord, slowly eating the youngest first, followed by the next one and the next one." He grinned hissing and sneering.

I breathed and glared at him deeply, "Well you don't know my wife!" In the blink of an eye, I cast him away as a burst of darkness flowed over me, pulsing and transforming me back into the demon like monster. My feet arched as claws formed once again, my muscles stretched as my body grew. I slammed my sword to the ground, it taking shape, as my body did, with a blood red soul. My hair turned black as my skin turned red and my scars glowed, my eyes glaring deep into his soul.

He laughed, "Oh I see. It seems I struck a nerve! Well guess what, no matter what you are or how strong you are, you will never beat me!"

A coat of black fire formed over his body, burning away his robe, making his black armor shine with fire, his hair flowed back like smoke. He stabbed his blade into the ground as the fire flowed into it making it grow and mutate into a huge black blade of hell.

"Here I come brother!" he charged me, blasting at me with the black raging flame. I knocked the fire away and knocked his blade away as he slashed relentlessly. He spun and kicked me across the face, "Ha! Gotcha!"

I tossed my blade in the air as I slammed my hand to the floor and used the force from his kick to spin my body and kick him hard into another frozen body "AAH!".

I caught my blade and kicked him once again, forcing his body through a frozen corpse statue and into the wall behind it.

As Drake shook off the blow, he asked, "Where are you getting so much power!? You were never anything close to this when we were younger!"

I wanted to say something but I couldn't, I just felt so angry.

"…not going to answer me?" he said. "Well then I'll just beat it out of you!" He grit his teeth as he stood to his feet and charged the black flame further.

Suddenly a look came upon his face… a look of a sick painful feeling came over him. "AH!…AAH!" his wounds popped and cracked as his body strained trying to hold in the black fire's power. His scars split and leaked smoke and fire. He cringed and stared at me, suddenly charged me, clashing hard with my blade, and knocked me back.

"You will die before me, there is no way I'm going to let you beat me!" He blasted massive bursts of black fire at me; I dodged over and over till finally, he hit me. But instead of pain and burns…I somehow absorbed the flame into my body through my own scars.

"What the…?" we both said as he slashed his blade down on mine, sparks flying from the clashing metal. I pushed back on my blade and tossed him back. He grunted and moaned as the fire seared his flesh.

"How does it feel?" I asked. "Feeling the pain… the burn of that flame for yourself? Hmm?!" The flames spat and popped his flesh.

"Shut up!… you know nothing of this power…" he said.

I glared as I felt a surge of heat through my arms and suddenly both black and red flames burst out and wrapped around my sword, hugging it with a casing of flame and steel.

I understood now, what was happening with the black fire. Drake had misused it, overpowered himself with it, and the black flame itself was choosing me to take it from him. It wanted me to be the holder of its power and fused itself with my soul to make sure I would succeed.

I looked to Drake. As he charged at me he yelled, "No! You're not going to take my power from me! And when I'm done with you, I'll kill everyone in your precious family with my power, one by one!"

I glared at him and in an instant I blacked out. When I opened my eyes, I could see what I was doing but I couldn't control myself. I smacked Drake away like a fly, my body hunched over like an animal, and I roared as my fangs gritted.

Drake stared at me, a little freaked out, "What the hell are you?!…"

I roared, cracking the ice with the sound. He stumbled to his feet and before he could even look up, I had him by the throat crushing it in my hand. I felt such a huge surge of blood lust. I raised him up as he kicked my chest over and over.

"Let go! Off me!" he gasped and stabbed his blade into my arm.

I couldn't feel a thing… I was so… numb. I looked at him, gritted my teeth, and threw him through a wall into a crystal room, then gouged into his back with my burning sword, shredding through his armor and flesh. He slammed into another statue and breathed hard as he felt the burn of the black fire. I felt so good; tilting my head slightly, I looked at the blade covered with blood.

He laughed at me, "Oh look at you, you're nothing but a crazed animal! You want to kill me! Huh! Do yah! Come on, kill me... KILL ME!"

Again, I lost all control, slamming my blade on the ground and roaring as I rushed at him. The fire on the blade gushed and grew. I raised the blade and slashed down.

"NO!" I suddenly heard a familiar voice and right before I obliterated Drake...

"Cloud... this is not who you are, come back to me... I love you..." A burst of smoke flowed over me, changing me back with a bright light pushing the darkness away. I felt at peace... as I gently floated back down and stood there staring at him. He was bleeding badly with spurts of fire bursting from his wounds.

He sighed and cringed as the pain surged through him, "Why... why did you stop...why didn't you kill me and rid this world of me?!" He spat blood at me hissing.

I stared at him, slowly relaxing, taking a deep breath keeping the voice of my wife in my head. I could feel the rage melting away as I raised the tip of my blade to his throat. He breathed harder forcing himself onto his feet.

"Say something!" he said frustrated with my silence.

He grabbed his sword from the ground and swung at me with the last of his strength. I easily stopped it with only two fingers, staring into his eyes still filled with hate.

"Brother, that monster that I was, is not me. Just like this is not you. What in the world started this? Why did you do this to our family... our people? All because of your selfish lust for power, you not only killed our lords, but you hurt our families, even dragging my own son down in your plan. You have probably completely wiped out both angel and vampire kind... I hope you're happy with what you have done because it will truly be the only thing you have ever done and failed at in your life."

His expression dimmed, his enraged face, previously filled with hate and anger... turned into depression and regret. The flames slowly died down and his pain stopped, his scars closed up, and he soon looked just like the brother I knew and cared about for so long. He sighed hard to himself and stared at me as his eyes went from black to blue and small tears pooled in his eyes.

"Brother... Cloud... I'm so sorry... for your family...for the gods... for everything... I'm so sorry Cloud..."

I placed my hand on his shoulder, "You have seen the error of your ways Drake. Now redeem yourself by helping us take Donovan down."

Tears rolled down his face as he pushed me away, "I can't accept your care and love, I don't deserve it... Cloud I'm going to die soon, you really knocked me a good one..." I wiped the sweat from his face.

He continued, "But now I will do the only thing I can to help you get our people, our world back. I will sacrifice my life... my soul to give you this power... the power of the black flame... it will be yours. Promise me you will use it to take back what is yours and once was mine. Promise me that you will get everything back that I messed up. Kill Donovan and get the world back to the way it was...no matter what."

I sighed as I looked into his eyes, his eyes that finally looked like his own. "I promise you Drake; I'll get back our world, and kill the mudak who made you become something you never were."

He held my hand tight as he pulled the tip of my blade to his stomach "If it truly chooses you, it will fight with you, protect you, and maybe in the end, you will be able to purify it and thus purify me." He then dropped his blade and placed both my hands on the sword holding them firm. I looked him in the eye as a tear fell.

"And Cloud... I'm sorry about Cross... I know in the end you'll be able to save him from Donovan's grip." I took a deep breath and then thrust my blade into him.

He smiled in relief as he passed away in peace. Then in a burst a black fire, his body turned from flesh and bone to a burning black flame, glowing as if light was shining through a black pearl.

A voice quickly came to me, "You might want to take a breath, Cloud."

I looked at the fire as it shined and flowed up the blade and fused into my body. I felt a massive surge of pain as the spirit flowed through me as if it was my very blood. My scars slowly closed and healed before my eyes. In an instant, I was healed and all my pain was gone.

I heard the voice again, "Quickly now, to the King!" I raised my head remembering Victor and Sam and darted away as fast as I could.

Victor and Sam watched as the Dark King rose from the crater.

"There is no way…" Sam said as he shivered. "Alright, that's it!" He pulled his gun from his jacket, popped it open and loaded in some sort of bluish bullet.

"Sam what are you doing?" Victor asked as they stepped back a little.

"I'm going to use one of the bullets I should of used this whole time… but I was really wanting to save these for something really big."

Victor's eyes widened a bit, "Big? How big?"

Sam closed the gun as he aimed, "About thirty stories." Victor stepped back a bit more bracing himself as Sam aimed.

He pulled the trigger and blue sparks spat from the gun as the bullet shot, giving off a tremendous shock wave. The Dark King was obliterated as the bullet passed through him and destroyed the entire wall behind him along with many rooms and hallways.

Victor smiled and yelled with joy, "Hell yeah! I can't believe it, you blew him into nothing but slime and blood! I mean a bullet that could take down a beast that's thirty stories tall?! Where did you get something like that?"

Sam laughed "Oh son, stop getting so excited, my grandson makes them. He loves his explosives and chemicals. The only bad thing is that they got one hell of a kick to them; if I'm not careful I can have my arm ripped clean off. I only have 8 more left on me but I can get some more when we get back to my home, if you want."

Victor laughed as well, "That would be a great treat, thanks Sam."

Suddenly… they heard a slithering, water like sound. They looked around.

"Where is it coming from…" They looked to each other and thought the same thing.

"No way…" Victor said, shaking his head and gritting his teeth as they turned to see the blood and organs somehow pulling themselves back together. Victor grew angry as the body soon formed back together, bringing the Dark King back to life.

"What the hell are you!" Victor yelled, as Sam stood there speechless.

I ran in to see the Dark King charging at Victor and Sam with his fists suddenly wielding great crystal like blades. I glared at the Dark King and quickly stepped in to clash with his crystal blades and knock him back with a strong force.

Victor said, "Cloud, whatever you're going to do, do it now!" I plunged my sword through his gut.

"AAHH!" he yelled as the blade tore him open. He looked at me with an evil stare.

"You're going to have to do better than that!" he said, coughing up blood and pulled the blade in deeper, piercing it through his body. I heard a voice as the Dark King got closer and closer with his crystal blade,.

"Cloud, say ignite, then send him home…"

I grinned and replied, "Thanks… brother."

The Dark King yelled in my face, "Your damn sword won't beat me!!" as he raised his blade.

I smiled in return, "Oh really?… ignite!"

Suddenly, the sword burst, flowing with the black fire, engulfing and turning the dark king into a black ball of fire. He screamed as he thrashed in pain. I lifted him up with the blade as if he was a stuck pig on a stick and threw him at the ice coffin, shattering it in a burst of blue and black smoke.

We all stood ready for what would rise from the smoke. We heard a moan, as a large figure rose from the dust and revealed that it was… the Old King… the True King, awake and with no darkness in him at all.

"What in the sweet snow is going on here!" He may have been awake and not evil but… he sure was really angry. "Well?! Why does my crystal chamber look like an ice giant just finished walking through?!"

Sam rushed over greeting him, "Oh thank the heavens you're awake and alright!"

The Old King smiled and hugged him tight, turning Sam's face blue, "Sam! It feels like I haven't seen you in ages!"

Sam slapped his shoulder, "Nick! Nick! Can't… breathe…"

Nick quickly let go as Sam coughed a little and caught his breath. "Oh I'm sorry Sam, it's just great to see you again old friend." They pat each other on the back.

"Now really… what happened to my home, Sam? Is this your doing?"

Sam scratched his head as he dusted off his hat, "Well that is a very interesting and long story, so, umm… how about we talk about it over dinner. Hmm?"

The King thought it through and smiled, "Ho! Ho! That's a great idea Sam, I feel like I could eat a whole snow ape! Ho! Ho! You and your friends are welcome."

A couple of small people walked into the room as if they were sick, "Wha… what happened sir?"

Nick laughed, "Ho! Ho! That's what I asked. Now gather up every one you can find in the castle. We're having a victory feast for my friends."

Sam sighed and whispered into Nick's ear "We really need to talk Nick…"

CH. 11
GETTING OUT

Back with the family... They started looking around and found a couple of torches. Shade lit one and suddenly the whole ruins were lit up with fire, shining like a city of gold. Everyone was mesmerized by its beauty.

Rossa asked "Mother what is this place?"

Sonja pondered, "I think this was once the home of the Angel God, when time first began. This must have been where he awoke for the first time."

Ellen responded, "That would explain why it's so shiny for a cave."

Shade sighed and looked to his mother, "Mom… what are we going to do anyway? I mean the gods are dead… dad's gone, probably also dead, and almost all of the vampire and angel races have been exterminated…what are we suppose to do now?"

Sonja look at her son with a bleak look on her face, "I'm not sure what we can do. All I know is that we are alive and we need to survive this. We need to meet up with any other survivors there may be and try to find out what happened to your father. Where he is, I have no idea. All I do know is that he is alive and that there is something wrong, something that was locked away that must have pushed itself out. I don't know where it could have come from, but we will find out, one way or another, and get him back."

Rossa sighed and walked through the ruins as the others followed, "What was wrong with him, was dad ok?"

Sonja stroked her baby girl's hair "I'm not really sure, but when I saw him last, he…"

Suddenly a crash sounded loudly from behind them along with a bright shining green light. They went toward the light, but soon heard the loud thumping of marching footsteps. Sonja pulled Rossa back into the dark as Shade pulled in Ellen. Hordes of vamperic demons marched though the ruins looting the gold and platinum.

"They must being looking for survivors" Rossa whispered.

Shade interrupted, "Looks more like they're just taking and killing whatever they can…"

Ellen asked, a little scared, "There are so many… how do we get out?"

The horde made their way to a wall and in their hands glowed fiery red balls.

Shade strained to see, "What are they doing?" All at once, they blasted at the wall, destroying it completely. A dim light shown into the cave...

Sonja took Rossa's hand as Shade took Ellen's, "That's our way out. Stay close and move quickly."

They watched for an opportunity to escape and carefully followed the looters through the wall and out. They slipped out behind the soldiers, climbed up, and hid themselves behind the jagged boulders atop the hill. They turned to see the land completely devastated as demonic armies marched across the dusty and jagged hills. Their eyes widened and filled with sadness; Shade sighed as the girls gasped lightly at the sight.

"The land... it used to be so beautiful... and now it's nothing but dust. What should we do?" Rossa asked wiping her eyes.

Sonja held her baby close, "All that we can do... is survive and wait for your father to return. If possible, do what we can to return this world back to the way it was before... to a land of beauty and peace. But first, we have to deal with the demons that turned what we loved into this waste land, into this world of death, and stop it at its source... Donovan..."

CH. 12
ST. NICK

Nick sighed rubbing his head, "What did I do... all I remember is seeing a man in black then nothing."

Sam patted his back, "You didn't do anything Nick. You were held against your will, trapped in that coffin of ice 'till we finally came along and broke you loose."

Nick stood from his chair and paced, "But that was still me, at least a part of me, roaming the land, torturing and killing the very people I cared so much for." He sat back in his chair rubbing his eyes.

Sam thought hard, "Think about it this way, Nick. You're back and in one piece, lucky to even be alive. The best thing to do now is to stop moping around and fix the land you love so dear. Rebuild it, re-arm yourselves, build up your armies and prepare for a war where we will need you to fight by our side and stop this madness from its source before it completely overruns us and wipes out every being that ever thought of creation instead of destruction as a means to make a better world. It's not just our world, it's their world," Sam said pointing to Cloud and Victor who were receiving medical attention.

"Those men somehow came here the same way the man in black came. That means their land is under more devastation than ours. We owe them our lives. If it wasn't for them, we would not be here right now. So, raise your armies, arm yourselves with every means of light you can, and wait for the day we go back with them and help them save their world as they are trying to save ours."

Victor stood up and objected, "Oh no you don't, I am only here because I'm with Cloud, there is no way we are going to save an entire world. We still have to get back to our world and kill that mudak father of mine who is turning it into a wasteland as we speak."

I stood and stopped him, "Victor, we need to help them."

Victor snapped, "Why?"

I raised my hand, "One, because we really need some allies right now. Two, we don't even know how to get back. And three, by the way, you say you're only here because of me. Thus, you will go wherever I go and whenever I say we go, so shut up, and come along. You will get to kick plenty of ass anyway."

Victor frowned, then laughed, "You got that right. I sure love to kick some ass. What are we waiting for? Let's get going."

Sam smiled, stood to his feet, and shook Nick's hand. "It seems we are moving on now, I still have to get back to my people, and you have your people to take care of again. Happy rebuilding friend."

Nick laughed, shaking Sam's hand in return, "Ho, Ho. You are right indeed. If you need anything, you tell us. We will try our best to get communications back up as soon as possible." He slapped Sam hard on the back.

Coughing, Sam smiled rubbing his shoulder, "You got it…"

Nick walked to Victor and I and shook our hands, "You two take real good care of Sam now, and thank you for all that you have done for us thus far."

We shook his hand in return, smiling, glad we could help, "We will sir. We do owe him for saving us from freezing to death so, you can count on us," Victor said quickly cutting in. "Now which way do we go?"

Nick walked over to his chair and opened up the desk back behind it. He dug around and pulled out a leather case. "There are many ways out of the Snow Land, but I would say the best way would be toward the southeast. You should run into the land of Green within the next day or two." He pulled out a map of the lands and gave it to Sam, "Follow Sam, he knows where to go better than anyone; he has been traveling and visiting me at least 5 times every year."

I looked to Sam and smiled, "Okay sir, it was great to meet you and I'm glad we were able to help. But sir, I can't leave without my father's things. Yes, I have my sword and guns but, I still need my father's jacket and glasses… any idea where they might be?"

Nick pondered and looked along the walls and cases, "Where would I keep them?…" he said quietly to himself as he pondered. Then it came to him as he spotted a tall black safe, "That's it! The forbidden armor!"

He rushed to it, worked several dials, and with all his might lifted up on a heavy leaver. He stood back as the door slowly opened, revealing that the dark armor was gone, but in its place was a folded up jacket with a pair of glasses on top. I saw him smile as he reached in, pulled them out, and handed them to me, "I believe these are what you were talking about?"

I smiled with relief and took them from him. "I was afraid that Drake had destroyed them," I said putting on the jacket and placing the glasses in the pocket.

He chuckled lightly and slapped my back, "It seems not… I'll assume the black forbidden armor is destroyed, since your brother was wearing it. One less thing for me to worry about," he said as he chuckled.

He then escorted us outside, "Take good care now. And don't forget to send word of when you're heading back to your World."

We shook his hand one last time, "We won't forget. Thank you and so long."

Victor smiled, jokingly saying, "Yeah, you keep this place under control now, no more crazy parties!"

Nick chuckled once more and waved as we left.

By the way... the King of the Land of White, now lacking evil of any kind, redeemed himself in the eyes of his people. He took such good care of them and the land, he was given a new name and was called a saint... Saint Nicholas.

"So Sam, where too?" I asked.

He pulled out the map and took a good look, "Like Nick said, the first stop is the land of Green. You will see it will get warmer real soon."

Victor sighed with relief, "Oh thank the gods, I've really gotten sick of the cold!"

"Well then, let's hurry up. The longer it takes to get out of the snow, the more we'll end up turning into ice statues," I said as I got to the top of a hill.

Looking out to see a thin line of green over the horizon, I thought of my family, "Sonja, take good care of yourself and make sure you and the kids are still there when I get back. I love you, and I'll be home soon…"

Appendix

Samuel Wilson, introduced in Chapter 5, is a reference/likeness to the Uncle Sam frequently shown on U.S. government posters. The real Samuel Wilson from Troy, New York, was a butcher who supplied meat to the American troops during the War of 1812. Legend is the meat was shipped in barrels marked "Uncle Sam's Butcher Shop." Eventually Uncle Sam became synonymous with the government. You can find more information on Uncle Sam at the library or on the Internet.

Notes

Notes

DEMON ALPHABET CODE

Solve This:

PRACTICE ON YOUR OWN....

PRACTICE ON YOUR OWN....

PRACTICE ON YOUR OWN....